THE CHARIOTEER

HUMANITY IS ALIVE?

ER. MANJU ASHISH BUDDHAGHOSH

Copyright © Er. Manju Ashish Buddhaghosh
All Rights Reserved.

This book has been self-published with all reasonable efforts taken to make the material error-free by the author. No part of this book shall be used, reproduced in any manner whatsoever without written permission from the author, except in the case of brief quotations embodied in critical articles and reviews.

The Author of this book is solely responsible and liable for its content including but not limited to the views, representations, descriptions, statements, information, opinions and references ["Content"]. The Content of this book shall not constitute or be construed or deemed to reflect the opinion or expression of the Publisher or Editor. Neither the Publisher nor Editor endorse or approve the Content of this book or guarantee the reliability, accuracy or completeness of the Content published herein and do not make any representations or warranties of any kind, express or implied, including but not limited to the implied warranties of merchantability, fitness for a particular purpose. The Publisher and Editor shall not be liable whatsoever for any errors, omissions, whether such errors or omissions result from negligence, accident, or any other cause or claims for loss or damages of any kind, including without limitation, indirect or consequential loss or damage arising out of use, inability to use, or about the reliability, accuracy or sufficiency of the information contained in this book.

Made with ♥ on the Notion Press Platform
www.notionpress.com

To My Esteemed Readers,

Dear Readers,

On this auspicious occasion of the publication of my story The Charioteers, I warmly welcome you all from the depths of my heart. This story is born not just from my life experiences but also from the diverse realities of society and the countless inspirations I have encountered along my journey. For me, this work is not merely a literary endeavor but a heartfelt call—a call that draws attention to humanity, friendship, and social harmony.

I would like to express my deepest gratitude to my family, friends, and the writing community, without whose support, encouragement, and guidance this story would not have been possible. I come from a humble family where I have learned social responsibility and sensitivity from my great-grandfather (Late Mr. Moti) and every member of my family. The environment at home has always inspired me with good thoughts, a positive outlook, and a strong sense of duty toward society.

I am especially thankful to my father, Dr. Ashish Kumar Gautam, who has been a great source of inspiration for my writing. His literary contributions, numerous national awards, and dedication to social reform have continually motivated me. My grandfather, Mr. Baburam Gautam, a retired principal, whose stories and social insights deeply influenced me, also deserves my heartfelt thanks. I am equally grateful to my mother, Mrs. Manju Gautam, my aunt Anusadhana Ji, my uncles Shri Agney Kumar Gautam and Ajey Kumar Gautam (Advocate), and my revered maternal grandfather (Late Mr. Munni Lal). The stories and teachings of my grandfather shaped my personality and made me a better human being.

I also thank my aunt Anamika Ji, Rinki Gautam Ji, Akashdeep Uncle, Kishan Uncle, Ajit 'Baba' Uncle, dear Anuj, Manju, Ashish, Budhyash, Animesh Pratap Singh, and my father for dedicating their precious time to review and provide feedback on the final draft of this story.

My sincere thanks to my publisher as well, who has given me the opportunity to bring this work to readers and helped me realize my dreams.

Through this story, I wish to convey that we are never truly alone on life's journey. Often, we do not realize who becomes our "Saarthi" (charioteer), guiding and supporting us at critical moments. Therefore, as much as possible, we should extend our help to others and move forward together. When we stand by each other, not only do we progress, but we also lead society toward a better future.

Finally, I sincerely thank all of you, dear readers, who will read my story and make it a part of your lives. Your support means the world to me, and I am proud to have you all.

With heartfelt gratitude,

- Manju Ashish Buddhaghosh

Contents

Foreword

It is a rare privilege as a father, a writer, and a teacher to witness the creative journey of one's own child. When I first read the short stories and watched the short films crafted by my son, Manju Ashish Buddhaghosh, I saw in him a sensitivity and depth that is the mark of a true storyteller. Today, as I pen the foreword to his book 'The Charioteers', I am filled with immense pride and hope.

The Charioteers is not just a story—it is a mirror to our society, reflecting both its fractures and its enduring possibilities for compassion. Through the intertwined lives of two friends from different religious backgrounds, the narrative explores the harsh realities of discrimination, caste, and communal divides, yet also celebrates the resilience of the human spirit and the redemptive power of friendship.

What sets this book apart is Buddhaghosh's ability to weave together the emotional and the philosophical, drawing from both personal experience and a keen observation of the world around him. His characters arc not mere figures on a page, but living embodiments of the struggles and hopes that define our times. The story's coincidences, its moments of pain and grace, and its honest questioning of social norms all invite readers to reflect on their own beliefs and actions.

Having spent my own life immersed in literature and social thought, and having been honored with national awards for my writing, I recognize in the Charioteers a rare sincerity and courage. Buddhaghosh does not shy away from difficult questions—he asks, through his narrative, whether religion alone defines us, or if humanity and empathy are the true measures of our worth.

This book is a timely reminder that, despite all our advancements, we still have far to go in the test of humanity. It urges us to look beyond the barriers of caste, creed, and prejudice, and to find in each other the "Charioteers"—the guide, the companion—who helps us navigate life's journey.

I congratulate Manju Ashish Buddhaghosh on this remarkable achievement. May 'The Charioteers' inspire every reader to become a charioteer of compassion and understanding in their own lives.

With pride and blessings,
Dr. Ashish Kumar Gautam
Writer, Teacher, Thinker, National Award Winner

Preface

I am deeply grateful for the opportunity to write this book, a journey that has been as transformative for me as I hope it will be for my readers. The Charioteers was born out of my personal experiences and observations of the world around me—a world often divided by boundaries of caste, creed, and circumstance, yet united by the universal values of compassion and friendship.

Throughout this journey, I have been blessed with the unwavering support and encouragement of my family. Their love and patience, especially during the most challenging times, have been my greatest strength and motivation to persevere.

My heartfelt thanks go to my friends and colleagues, whose valuable feedback and insights helped me refine my thoughts and improve the overall quality of this book. I am also sincerely grateful to the experts in this field who generously shared their knowledge and expertise, enriching the content of this work.

I would like to express my appreciation to my publisher and the entire team for their professionalism, guidance, and dedication in bringing this book to fruition.

Above all, I am thankful to everyone who has been a part of this endeavor. Any shortcomings in this work are solely my own, and I hope that readers will find value and inspiration within these pages.

Thank you for joining me on this journey. May the Charioteers encourage you to look beyond differences and become a guiding companion in someone else's life.

Acknowledgements

Writing this story has been a unique journey of the heart, and it would not have been possible without the support and encouragement of many wonderful people.

First and foremost, I express my deepest gratitude to the real-life inspirations behind my characters:

Anuj Vimal: This name comes from my engineering friend, whose full name is actually 'Anuj Vimal.' He is someone who always stands by his word—if he says, "I'll do it" or "I'll wait for you," he truly means it. His loyalty, friendship, and reliability helped shape this character.

Hamza: This character is inspired by a colleague and good friend from my first workplace. Hamza's simplicity, honesty, and friendship have always been a source of inspiration for me.

Ramvilas: The name is taken from my father's childhood friend. I have heard countless stories from my father about their friendship—how they protected each other from teachers and mischievous students during school days, supported each other in studies, and how Ramvilas joyfully celebrated my father's achievement as a gold medalist in D.Pharm. Their friendship has always been an ideal for me.

Pandit Ji and Maulana Sahab: These characters were inspired by people I saw in Ayodhya, where religious politics were at a peak. Yet, these two representatives of different religions would meet daily, share a cup of tea, and polish their friendship. I witnessed how they spoke about humanity and stood by each other beyond religious divides. Their friendship taught me the true meaning of harmony and coexistence.

I am also deeply thankful to my family and friends for their unwavering belief in this project. Your patience, love, and encouragement fueled me during moments of doubt and exhaustion.

Special thanks to the community leaders, social workers, and educators who tirelessly work to bridge divides and foster understanding. Your dedication to humanity's betterment inspired many themes explored in this narrative.

I extend my heartfelt appreciation to the editors, reviewers, and mentors who offered invaluable feedback and helped shape this manuscript into what it is today. Your insights and guidance have been instrumental.

Finally, I thank every reader who opens this book with an open mind and heart. May this story inspire compassion, reflection, and a commitment to stand together as charioteers on life's journey.

With gratitude,

Yours sincerely,

Manju Ashish Buddhaghosh

thbuddhaghosh@gmail.com, +919918293747

Prologue

In this story, inspired by the many facets of life, we witness the journey of two friends who, knowingly or unknowingly, are forced to confront challenges that stand in stark opposition to the very idea of humanity. This is a tale of friendship spanning two generations, aiming to strike at the growing divisions in society and hold up a mirror to our collective conscience. Discrimination—whether based on color, social status, religion, or caste—is always wrong. When nature itself made no distinction in creating us, and provided us all with the same resources for life—air, water, sunlight—then why do we, as mere humans, create such divisions?

The story places a special emphasis on the religious notions prevalent in society, raising the question: Is religion everything? Is there no value in humanity and compassion?

The character of Hamza is that of a simple, honest man who makes a living through small jobs. He is not highly educated. Much like the many people from Uttar Pradesh and Bihar who leave their homes to earn a living in big cities like Delhi and Mumbai, the other main character, Ramvilas, also works as a daily wage laborer. Through their stories, you will witness the lives of two men—one Hindu, one Muslim—shaped by man-made religious divisions.

This narrative attempts to comment on the evils of colorism, casteism, and religious discrimination in society. In the second part, through the characters of Anuj and Vimal, the story explores the coincidences of nature and time. It also reflects on how a priest and a maulvi see each other, offering a glimpse of true harmony.

I hope this story resonates with you and inspires reflection.

CHAPTER ONE

THE CHARIOTEER'S COINCIDENCE

In a poor Muslim household, there was an air of great happiness. Hamza's wife was expecting, and the family was eagerly awaiting the arrival of good news. Hamza's mother was quite elderly, and he was her only son—born after many prayers and hopes, at a time when his parents had almost given up on having children. Now, his mother wished for nothing more than to see her grandson's face before departing for her heavenly abode, for Hamza's father had passed away in an accident just a few days earlier. The family's situation was far from stable.

After his father's passing, Hamza was engulfed in sorrow. His worries deepened as both his mother's and wife's health showed no signs of improvement. To make matters worse, his wife had received two life-altering pieces of news at once: she was pregnant, and she had cancer.

About three months later, the doctor brought a glimmer of hope—there was some improvement in his wife's condition. But if they truly wanted her to recover, she would need therapy, which would require a significant amount of money. Determined to save his wife, Hamza began working tirelessly. He did odd jobs at the local merchant's house during the day, but the earnings were meager.

One night, as he was passing by the rice mill's warehouse, Hamza noticed two men loading sacks onto a truck. Suddenly, one of the men slipped while lifting a sack, fell, and broke his leg.

Fig: Ramvilas and others loading goods from the warehouse onto the truck.

People from nearby rushed over, but only the two men loading the sacks were laborers; the rest were workers engaged in other tasks—some were machine operators who soon returned to their stations. Hamza saw the injured man writhing in pain, but the clerk standing there was shouting, more concerned about the work. Hamza overheard him saying, "This shipment was supposed to be loaded and delivered today, but now that seems impossible."

At that moment, Hamza stepped forward and pleaded with the clerk to give him a chance. The clerk, focused solely on getting the job done, agreed without hesitation. Without wasting a moment, Hamza threw himself into the work with all his strength.

It took him quite some time to finish, and meanwhile, his wife back home was growing anxious, worrying about why he hadn't returned yet and what might have happened. When Hamza finally received his payment for the night's labor, he set aside half of it for the injured man—the very person because of whom he got the job. Hamza thought to himself, "Just as I need money, who knows, maybe he needs it even more now. With his leg broken, the poor fellow might not be able to work for a long time."

Ram Vilas was a very kind-hearted man, though his circumstances were not much better. When he broke his leg, he became deeply troubled. Lying behind the hospital curtains in the darkness, he saw a bearded man approaching and, for a moment, was frightened—wondering if his time had come and Yama, the god of death, had arrived to take him away. But as Hamza came closer and asked about his well-being, Ram Vilas remembered that the man who had brought him to the hospital after his accident was none other than this same person.

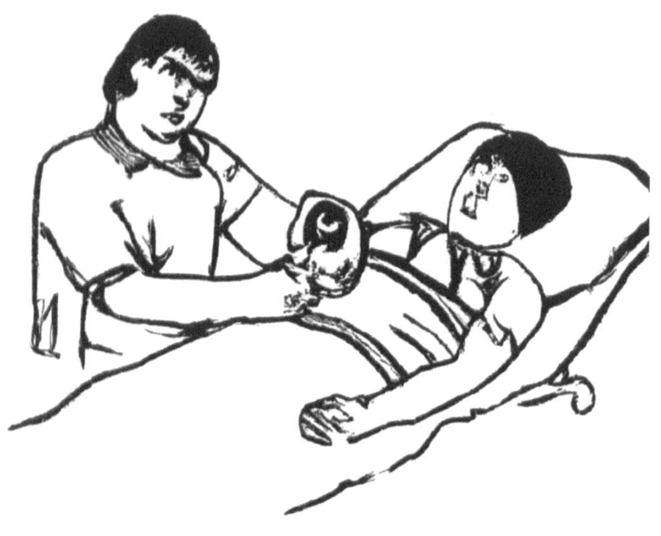

fig: Hamza giving Ramvilash his share of the money at the hospital.

Hamza had some money in his hand and was saying something. As Ram Vilas listened carefully, he heard Hamza say that if Ram Vilas hadn't been injured, Hamza wouldn't have gotten the job, nor the money, nor would the two of them have met. Hamza expressed his gratitude to Ram Vilas, sharing his own story. When Hamza mentioned that he was soon to become a father, it was as if two brothers, separated at a fair, had finally reunited. In just a few moments, they became so close that it felt as if they had known each other for years.

With a heavy heart, Ram Vilas shared his own sorrow: "I am also unfortunate. I, too, am about to become a father, but in this condition—how will I take care of my wife? Just a few days ago, my wife joyfully shared the news that we were expecting, and now here I am, lying on a hospital bed."

Hamza replied, "Brother, I got this work only because of you. If you don't mind, I'd like to help carry your burden until you recover." Despite Ram Vilas's repeated refusals, Hamza insisted. It was his sense of dignity and humanity. The two became the closest of friends, visiting each other's homes, sharing meals, and spending time together.

This newfound friendship between a Hindu and a Muslim did not sit well with the so-called respected members of society. They could not understand how such a bond was possible. But fate had its own plans. Hamza was blessed with a son, but due to his mother's internal illnesses, the child was born a dwarf. Within a few days, Hamza's wife bid farewell to this sorrowful world; later, the doctor revealed that she had been in the final stages of cancer. Before Hamza could recover from this grief, his mother too closed her eyes forever. He was left all alone, with his infant son, who was only a few months old.

Meanwhile, violence in the name of religion was spreading across the country—not just in cities, but now even in villages. People were ready to kill each other over being Hindu or Muslim. It all began with a simple incident: "A Muslim child drank water from a pot kept at a temple." On a scorching May-June afternoon, the boy saw a cow suffering from thirst. As he walked by, he noticed the cow stumble and collapse. Nearby, he saw a bucket outside the priest's room in the temple. He picked it up, filled it with water, and saved the cow's life.

After climbing up and down the stairs, the boy grew tired and sat down under a shady tree in the temple courtyard. Seeing this, a man felt pity for him, offered him some water, and told the priest everything that had happened. When it came to light that the boy was Muslim, the very same man who had felt pity raised a commotion and gathered a crowd, shouting that a Muslim had touched the priest's water pot. The people beat the poor boy so severely that he died right there.

*fig :*The crowd beating (or attacking) the child.

The news spread like wildfire. As a result, the villagers began to look at Hamza with suspicion and hostility, and some even waited for an opportunity to harm him. Yet, the friendship between Ram Vilas and Hamza remained unchanged. Hamza's son considered Ram Vilas's wife as his own mother, and she treated him like her own child. Hamza was known for making delicious murg musallam. Having lost his wife due to his inability to care for her health, he now made sure to look after his friend's wife. Whenever he cooked something special, he would cradle his beloved son in one arm and carry a food container in the other, heading straight to Ram Vilas's house.

Ram Vilas's brothers did not like this at all. Although they had divided their property and lived separately, barely speaking to each other, they still disapproved of Hamza's close bond with Ram Vilas.

A few days later, Ram Vilas also became a father. But fate played its cruel game—though the baby was born healthy, it soon became apparent that the child could not see. On the sixth day after the birth, when Ram Vilas's sister came to visit, his other brothers told her lies about Hamza and urged her to warn Ram Vilas. She said, "Muslims know black magic; he must have done something." This rumor reached Hamza, and he was deeply hurt. He stopped visiting Ram Vilas's house and devoted himself entirely to his child.

Meanwhile, the villagers poisoned Ram Vilas's mind with more lies and accusations. They even went so far as to claim that Hamza had an illicit relationship with Ram Vilas's wife, which was why he kept bringing her food. Hearing this, Ram Vilas could not bear it any longer. After two days of inner turmoil, he confronted Hamza, and their argument escalated to the point of a physical fight.

At the same time, Hindu-Muslim riots were spreading into the villages. Instead of calming the situation, radio and TV debates only fueled the fire, stirring up even more hatred.

Suddenly, Ram Vilas's wife began to bleed heavily—barely a month had passed since the birth of their child, and her condition was worsening day by day. People began to whisper that since Ram Vilas had attacked Hamza the previous day, Hamza must have used some kind of black magic, and that was why his wife was suffering now. The atmosphere in the village became so charged that Ram Vilas was forced to believe these rumors. He joined the villagers in storming Hamza's house and beating him mercilessly, refusing to listen to a word Hamza said. Hamza kept asking what had happened, why they were doing this to him, but no one listened. His child, lying on the bed, screamed and cried, perhaps sensing that his father would not survive. The villagers beat Hamza just as they had beaten the boy at the temple for drinking water. Hamza did not survive.

When Ram Vilas returned home, he found his wife missing and the baby crying. He began searching for her frantically, and blood stains led him to the road, where someone told him, "A woman in critical condition was just taken from here to the nearby hospital. There's little hope for her survival, poor thing!"

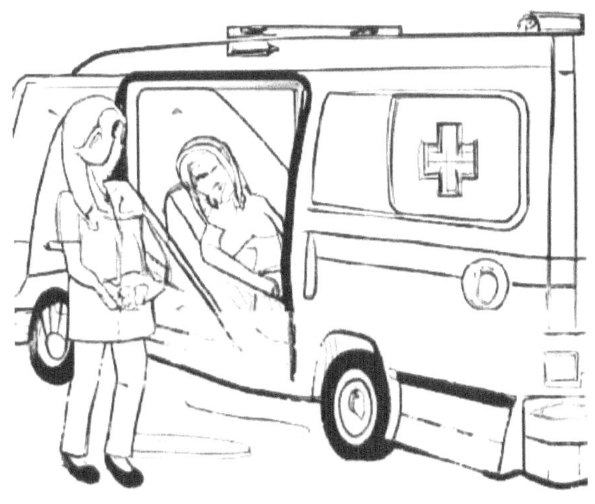

*fig:*The hospital vehicle taking Ramvilas's wife to the hospital.

He was filled with confusion and regret, tormented by the thought that he had raised his hand against Hamza, and that the villagers had attacked him so brutally. Hamza had stood by him through every hardship—what had he done in return? At the same time, he was consumed by anxiety: how would he face his wife now, knowing that he hadn't stood by her in her most vulnerable moment, and that his absence had led to this tragedy? Summoning all his courage, he entered the hospital room, only to find his wife breathing her last.

When she asked what had happened, Ram Vilas told her everything—from the lies his sister and the villagers had spread, to how they blamed Hamza for her condition, claiming Muslims practiced black magic. He confessed that he had gone to confront Hamza, had struck him, and then the villagers had beaten him to death. As he recounted all this, he forgot that Hamza had once been his dearest friend and all that Hamza had done for him; in that moment, he simply didn't want to appear at fault in front of his dying wife.

After hearing all this, Vilas's wife began to weep. In her final moments, she said—

"Hamza Bhai always treated me like his little sister. Just as I care for his son, he cared for me like an elder brother. He did everything he could to ease any pain I had. Ever since he stopped going to work, he spent his free time thinking only about Khalil (Hamza's son) and our soon-to-be-born child. He would often say, 'Khalil will never be alone now—he'll go to school and play with his brother, and I will give them all the happiness that Khalil's mother wanted for him, and that we ourselves never had in our childhood.'

He gave me two piggy banks—one for our child, and one for Khalil—and every day, he would put something in each, dividing it equally. After his wife passed away, he was often deeply sad and blamed himself, thinking that if he had cared for her better, maybe she would still be alive. That's why he took such special care of us, too.

Besides, don't you remember that when times were hard, and no relatives stood by us, it was Hamza who did? I told him many times not to trouble himself, but he would say, 'If my sister is well, my nephew will be well too.'

And what has happened to your understanding? That kind man, who always treated us with respect, was more than family to us—he was even more than a blood relative."

Hearing this, Vilas felt shattered inside and was filled with deep regret for the terrible mistake he had made. Just then, his wife's breathing grew heavier. With her last breath, she expressed her wish to see both children and Hamza Bhai one last time.

Vilas was at a loss—how could he leave his wife in this condition, and even if he went, how could he face Hamza? He vaguely remembered how Hamza's child had been wailing, but at the time, he hadn't felt a shred of pity. He hadn't uttered a single word to stop the mob from beating Hamza, let alone tried to help.

Vilas's remorse was unending. His wife's condition grew more critical, and he was torn between staying by her side and going to see the children and Hamza. In her final moments, his wife held Vilas's hand and said, "Promise me, you will never let either of the children suffer, no matter what—no matter if it costs you your life or mine..."

Suddenly, a heavy silence filled the room, as if time itself had stopped. The ticking of the clock grew louder. Vilas felt his own heartbeat slow—perhaps his wife was no longer in this world.

Vilas was left hollow inside. He watched, numb, as his wife was taken away for her last rites. He felt lifeless. The villagers and relatives performed the funeral, but Vilas had no awareness of where the children were or how they were doing; it was as if his soul had departed with his wife. In those days, the neighbors took care of the children.

One day, Vilas suddenly left home and never returned. Evening fell. When the neighbors heard the child crying alone in the house, they took care of him and tried to comfort him. As Vilas did not come back, people searched for him and spread the word among the nearby villages, asking anyone who saw Vilas to let him know that his child was in distress. After several days with no news, they took his child to an orphanage, since he was blind. After all, even broken things aren't kept at home, and here was a blind boy who didn't even realize what kind of trial fate had put him through.

The day Hamza was left bloodied and battered, people thought he was as good as dead and abandoned him. But his internal injuries had already stolen his last breath. That day, his son Khalil, crying and crawling on his knees, was too afraid to approach his father. Covered in blood, Hamza was almost unrecognizable. Khalil crawled away, sobbing, searching for his father out on the road. The gardener at the orphanage saw the boy crawling along the path, picked him up, and asked around to find out whose child he was, but everyone denied knowing him. The gardener gave him a new name—Anuj. He grew fond of the boy and spent hours playing with him. After a few days, the child's health improved, but his growth did not. One day, when the gardener learned that the boy was Muslim and, on top of that, a dwarf, he took him to the orphanage and left him there.

Ram Vilas, meanwhile, had lost his mind. Driven mad by the loss of his friend and wife, he became oblivious to the world—he forgot not only the promise he had made to his wife, but even that he had a child at all.

On the day of the naming ceremony at the orphanage, the children were named for their personalities and nature. Hamza's son, small and chubby, was called Anuj. Vilas's child, three months younger than Anuj but innocent by nature and blind from birth, was called Vimal.

Fate played its game—once again, Ram Vilas and Hamza lived on through their children. Hindu, Muslim, Sikh, Christian—an orphanage is the one place where no one asks for proof of religion. Anuj and Vimal became close friends—or rather, brothers. The very society that had cast them out as Hindu and Muslim now saw them growing up together under the roof of humanity.

Because they were different, the other children at the orphanage didn't want to talk to them, or even look at them. Gradually, Anuj and Vimal grew close, becoming each other's complement: Anuj grew older but his legs did not; Vimal, on the other hand, was blind from birth. In time, Vimal became Anuj's legs, and Anuj became Vimal's eyes.

CHAPTER TWO

THE FLOW OF LOVE

They say children are mischievous by nature—no one exemplifies this better than Lord Krishna himself. But the environment has a direct impact on children, and I firmly believe that if a child is raised during the era of the Mahabharata, he will always see himself as a warrior on a battlefield. If he is raised in the time of Buddha, there would hardly be any need to teach him virtue. A newborn child, until he is old enough to understand anything, absorbs the atmosphere around him. If he grows up in a family where members are constantly at odds, where egos prevail ("What I say is the only truth, nothing else in the world matters"), then as the child matures, he too will develop an ego. I say all this because if an ordinary person, by merely tasting alcohol at a friend's urging, can become a drunkard, then children—who are like blank slates—can be shaped into anything you wish.

In the orphanage, there were children with the innocence of Buddha and the fierceness of the Mahabharata. Anuj and Vimal still didn't fully understand what had happened to them. There were also children who had arrived at the ages of eight or ten—some showed tendencies of violence, others were as selfish as Kaikeyi. Such children did not like having a blind child and another whose height never increased among them. All the kids would gang up and mock them. If it weren't for Anuj, they might have hurt Vimal badly—sometimes pushing him into bushes, sometimes throwing him into water.

*fig:*Children running away after seeing a snake.

One day, a snake entered the orphanage, unaware that it had wandered among children more venomous than itself. That very day, a doctor couple came to the orphanage office to adopt Vimal. The manager's words and Vimal's gentle nature impressed them greatly. Being one of the consulting doctors, the man also knew that Vimal's blindness could be treated successfully.

When Anuj heard that Vimal might be adopted, he sat alone in a corner, lost in thought about what would become of him after Vimal left. Just then, a handful of children spotted the snake and ran away, but Anuj didn't notice what was happening. His foot was about to land on the snake when Vimal's voice broke his reverie. Looking down, Anuj saw the snake right in front of him. Without fear, he grabbed it and flung it away like a rope. Overcome with emotion, Anuj hugged Vimal tightly. Vimal couldn't understand why Anuj was behaving this way.

Vimal asked, "What's gotten into you today? Why so much love? Are you going somewhere?" But the truth was, it was Vimal who was about to be adopted, not Anuj.

Anuj then told Vimal everything and started crying, "Brother, will I never grow up? People taunt me, even the younger kids hit me, and today, those who came to adopt me..." He fell silent, remembering how the previous visitors had treated him with outright contempt, almost as if they'd slapped him. Vimal had no idea that anyone would ever want to adopt either of them.

Anuj sobbed, "Brother, I don't want to go anywhere. I just want to stay with you. No one understands me except you." Vimal tried to comfort him, "I'm blind, no one will ever take me. But your life will change if you go with them. They'll give you nice clothes and good food. Trust me, you should go, brother." Saying this, Vimal hugged Anuj, still unaware that the adoption was actually for him.

Anuj was quiet for a while, then explained the whole situation to Vimal. Hearing this, Vimal too became emotional and began to cry. Anuj comforted him, "There's no need for you to cry, Vimal. Sooner or later, we would have had to part—either I would go, or you. I'm lucky that I get to spend a few more days here, to enjoy with everyone. Don't worry about me. If life wills it, we'll meet again someday, and by then, you'll be able to see me, and you won't need anyone's help."

Vimal replied, "I'll pray to God that my brother too finds a good family, one that never troubles him and loves him like their own child."

But fate had other plans. The husband wanted to adopt Vimal, but the wife preferred Anuj. And when even gods must yield to goddesses, what chance did the doctor have? They decided to adopt Anuj. The lady had no idea that the child was a dwarf. When the time came to take him home, the manager packed Anuj's belongings and told him to get ready. Both children were left stunned.

Vimal said, "Didn't I tell you, Anuj? One day, a good family would come and take you as their own." Hearing this, Anuj broke down in tears. "Brother, you mustn't cry now. If you say goodbye with tears, how will I manage here alone? As for me, I've heard that there are schools now even for children like us. And from tomorrow, a teacher will come to the orphanage just to teach me," he added with a forced smile. "In a few days, when I'm ready, I'll go to that school too, and one day, we'll surely meet again somewhere."

Vimal's sadness was evident, and seeing him, Anuj also began to cry. The two became so emotional that they sat together, weeping. Because of some paperwork, Anuj couldn't take Vimal to the doctor himself. That day's events had left them both with a deep fear of separation. At mealtime, if Vimal was nowhere to be seen, Anuj would panic. Unable to find him, he would return to his room without eating, lost in thought—'Who would ever adopt this blind boy?' He would curse God, "Oh God, why did you make me blind? And if you had to, why didn't you at least give me my parents? If I sinned so much in my past life, why did you let me be born at all? And if you did, you could have taken me away at birth." And he would cry loudly.

Just then, Anuj would come in, see him crying, and ask, "What's wrong, Vimal? Why are you crying?" Vimal wouldn't say anything, but when Anuj asked him to come eat, he would go along. After much persuasion, he would eat a little, but the pain of being blind haunted him. His only friend would soon be adopted, and he would be left alone. This thought tormented him for days. Neglecting himself, his health deteriorated, and he had to be taken to the hospital.

The doctor was very kind. He gently tried to reason with Vimal, "If you don't eat, how will your friend manage without you? What if he falls ill too?" Vimal had grown so weak that he had to be hospitalized for two days.

This doctor was none other than the same one who had once come to the orphanage with his wife to adopt a child.

Meanwhile, Anuj was left alone. The other children, seeing him by himself, bullied him even more, making him realize just how incomplete he was without Vimal. He worried constantly about how Vimal would manage without him. He begged the warden to let him see Vimal, but the warden put him off, saying Vimal was fine now and would be back by morning.

The warden went to the hospital. During a conversation, the doctor told the warden that he had examined Vimal's eyes and was confident that Vimal would be able to see. The doctor explained that if two more tests, ordered by a senior doctor, came back positive, Vimal would regain his sight completely.

The warden was overjoyed, but the very next moment, he was troubled by the thought of how they would afford the treatment. Noticing the warden's concern, the doctor said, "If you allow, my NGO can help this child. I will cover all the expenses for his treatment."

Hearing this, the warden's eyes filled with tears of joy. He folded his hands in gratitude, "If there were more people like you in this world, humanity would never lose. Thank you so much—I can never repay your kindness."

"If you permit," the doctor continued, "I would like to adopt this child. That would be the greatest favor you could do for me. And, if you don't mind, I'd also like to take your children to a camp from time to time, so they can become mentally stronger and better understand the world."

Saying this, the doctor placed his hands over the warden's joined palms. The warden was so moved, it was as if he had seen God himself. Overjoyed and full of hope, he returned to the orphanage.

"Where is Vimal, Guruji? You said he would come today. Where is he? Please tell me, please!" Anuj, barely reaching the warden's knees, was tugging at him, asking anxiously. The warden, well aware of the brotherly bond between the two, gently explained, "Vimal will be able to see now, Anuj. The doctor said he will take Vimal to a better place where the world's best doctors will work together to treat his eyes. The doctor promised that after Vimal's operation, he'll bring him back, and take all of you on trips—not just once, but every year. By then, Vimal will also be able to see, and you'll all get to go to wonderful places together." Hearing this, Anuj was happy, but the sorrow of being separated from his friend lingered. He couldn't sleep all night—one moment he was overjoyed that his friend would see, the next he was sad that maybe he would never see Vimal again. He tried to console himself, thinking that when he grew up and left the orphanage, he would definitely go find Vimal.

At dawn, the warden began preparing the adoption documents. Thanks to the doctor's hard work, the reports were positive, and the operation was scheduled. The surgery went well, and a few weeks later, another report confirmed the success—only one last report remained. The doctor was confident it would be fine too. When the bandages were removed, Vimal said he could see, but only as if through a haze. The final report arrived, and the doctor realized he might have acted too quickly. That one report changed everything: Vimal was diagnosed with lymphoma and myeloma—a rare disease, the same one Anuj's mother had suffered from. In this illness, blood clots form throughout the body, increasing the risk of cancer in organs like the lungs, uterus, stomach, and intestines. Perhaps a clot formed during surgery, causing the hazy vision. Vimal could see, but for how long was uncertain; if the clot persisted, cancer could develop.

The doctor rushed to Vimal, where another doctor had just removed his bandages. "Vimal, can you see me?" he asked.

"Yes, but I see something strange. When I look at the door, there's a round, dark spot the same color as the medicine," Vimal replied.

The doctor took Vimal home. His wife accepted Vimal, but she wasn't truly happy—she had wanted her own child. The doctor taught Vimal, showing him colors and objects, answering his endless questions: "What is this? What do you call that?" Vimal, seeing everything for the first time, was full of curiosity. Sometimes, the doctor's wife would lose her patience with him. One day, Vimal mentioned he saw a red shadow everywhere. Tests revealed it was a blood clot, and over time, it began to steal his sight again. Just as he was entering his teens, his vision faded completely in a matter of months. Only one eye had been treated successfully, and now the other required surgery, but the chances were slim. Vimal could see with just one eye, which is why the doctor's wife never really liked him. She only cared for him because of her husband; otherwise, she acted more blind than Vimal himself. Eventually, Vimal lost his sight completely, and the doctor's wife's cruelty crossed all limits. When the doctor was away, she did as she pleased, but the moment he returned, she would shower affection on Vimal. The doctor believed his wife loved the boy deeply, unaware of her true behavior during the day.

One day, when the doctor returned home late, he didn't see Vimal and asked his wife about him. She replied that Vimal was sleeping in his room. Hearing this, the doctor ate, rested, and went to bed. But when Vimal was still nowhere to be seen the next morning, the doctor began searching for him. When he asked his wife again, she snapped, "He must be around here somewhere—where could a blind boy go?" This angered the doctor, and he scolded her harshly. Later, the household staff revealed that Vimal hadn't been seen at home for the past two days. The doctor, frantic, started searching the city for Vimal—"Poor boy, who knows what's become of my Vimal? What kind of witch did I leave him with? If I'd known, I would never have left him, or I'd have taken him with me wherever I went." His words seemed to burn his wife with shame, but she couldn't contain herself and retorted, "Let the blind boy go—good riddance to a burden."

At this, the doctor's anger exploded, and in a fit of rage, he struck his wife. "May he never be found, may he die, may he rot in hell!" she screamed, packing her bags and heading for her parents' home. She felt no pain or remorse for the loss of a helpless child. The doctor was heartbroken, wandering the city as if he had committed a grave sin, blaming himself for everything.

*fig:*The doctor telling the police inspector about Vimal.

When he could find no trace of Vimal, the doctor went to the police station and gave a full report: "There's a boy who wears a gold 'Om' pendant around his neck and cannot see." Months passed with no news. In his grief for Vimal, the doctor eventually remembered his promise to take the orphanage children on an outing. He took leave from the hospital and met with the warden to prepare for the trip. Meanwhile, Anuj had been looking for a chance to run away from the orphanage, and this was the perfect opportunity. On the second day of camp, Anuj escaped. No one at the orphanage seemed to care about his absence.

After being separated from Vimal, Anuj had become rebellious. The other children teased and bullied him relentlessly. When the warden was around, the other kids would act innocent while Anuj, unable to control his frustration, would lash out, earning a reputation as a troublesome and wicked child in the warden's eyes. He would hit anyone, break anything, and his mental state deteriorated day by day. So, when he finally ran away, no one was bothered in the least.

> *"If you find no value in a place, or cannot value it yourself, it is wiser to walk away. In leaving, you honor the dignity of both yourself and that place."*

Change is the law of nature. There was once the time of 'Buddha', who, sensing the evils that had seeped into society, withdrew from this world filled with greed and sorrow to seek refuge in nature. There are many noble and powerful things present in society, but society itself is slow to accept any kind of change.

People looked at Anuj with disdain because of his short stature—he remained a dwarf. People didn't even want to look at him. Even though he had studied at the orphanage, whenever he took his documents to apply for a job, people wouldn't even let him sit beside them because of his height.

Because his arms and legs were small, whenever someone gave him something, they treated him almost like an untouchable. One day, he overheard the vegetable vendor telling the neighboring shopkeeper, "Have you seen his hands? If you touch him, you'll catch leprosy too."

"Society measures a person's stature not by their character or personality, but by their wealth and possessions, even if that person, in terms of character and personality, is not just small but completely mired in the mud."

All these things eventually forced Anuj's landlord to evict him from his home. After being thrown out, Anuj made a derelict, abandoned house his new shelter. He chose that ruin because people believed it was haunted, and so no one ever went near it.

One night, Anuj was startled awake by the sound of dogs barking. For a few moments, he lay frozen in the silence. After a while, he stepped outside and saw a strange creature—its form somewhat human, yet not quite. The cold winter night was thick with fog, making the figure appear even more ghostly. Anuj was so frightened he couldn't even call out. Quietly, he tiptoed back inside and tried to sleep again.

In the morning, he woke to find a man shivering from the cold, groaning in pain. The man's body was covered in dog bites, and he wore several torn layers of clothing, one on top of the other. It seemed he couldn't see, for when Anuj called out, the man looked around, trying to sense where the voice was coming from. He was clearly anxious, searching for something with his hands. When Anuj reached out to comfort him, the man flinched, as if he had been mistreated many times before. Gently, Anuj reassured him that he meant no harm and helped him up, taking him to his humble abode and sharing whatever little food he had.

If you were dying of thirst in a desert and suddenly found a pond, it would feel like heaven; you'd be ready to jump in without a second thought, even if you didn't know how to swim. That's how hungry the blind man was—just like a lost wanderer in the desert who finds water. In his desperation, he ate half his food and spilled the rest. Watching him, Anuj was reminded of his childhood friend Vimal, who had once eaten in the same hurried, messy way when he'd heard the news of Anuj's adoption.

Anuj took great care of the man, seeing in him the shadow of his friend Vimal. With timely medicine and care, the man soon recovered. To pay for the medicines, Anuj did odd jobs in the market, earning just enough for food and treatment. The two became good friends, but neither had yet shared their names or stories.

One day, the blind man sat quietly, lost in thought, tears glistening in his eyes as he remembered his past. Seeing this, Anuj said, "Hey brother, why are you so sad? Look at me—people say all sorts of things about me, but I'm still happy!"

> *"In life, you cannot move forward even a single step if you pay attention to what people say. True wisdom lies in pursuing your goals without listening to the opinions of others."*

Responding to Anuj's words, Vimal said, "Why would people taunt you, brother? You're such a good person, always thinking of others' well-being. Why should you have to hear taunts? I'm the blind one, but people don't even want to lay eyes on me."

Hearing this, Anuj's pain spilled over. "Who would be happy to see a dwarf like me? Wherever I go, people won't even do anything—good or bad—after seeing me. Even a black cat is luckier than I am; if it crosses someone's path, they might hesitate, but eventually, they still go about their business. But after seeing me, people just abandon their plans for the day altogether."

There was a moment of silence. Then Vimal asked his name. Anuj replied in a low voice, "Are you going to make fun of me for being a dwarf too? The whole world does—will you join them?"

Vimal said, "No, brother! When I was a child, I lived in an orphanage. I had a friend there whom everyone called Chotu, Tingoo, Baingan, Bhanta, and all sorts of names."

Anuj, surprised, asked, "What? Orphanage? You lived in an orphanage too? Did you run away from there as well? I bet people troubled you too. I had to break a few heads to get out—they tormented me so much, those scoundrels."

Vimal replied, "No, brother, I didn't run away from the orphanage." He explained that he had been adopted by a good family. But Anuj couldn't believe it. "I was perfectly fine as a child, but no one adopted me. Why would anyone adopt a blind boy?"

Anuj pressed, "But you just mentioned the orphanage—so how did you end up in a home?"

Vimal explained, "Yes, I was raised in an orphanage, but I couldn't stay in the home where I was adopted. I had a friend named Anuj, whom I loved dearly—he was my eyes. One day, someone came to adopt him, and he told me about it. Maybe he's happy now. I pray every day that my brother is in a good place. Oh, and yes, I fell ill and went to the hospital, and after that, I never saw my friend again."

Hearing this, Anuj leapt forward and hugged Vimal tightly, sobbing uncontrollably. Vimal began to feel his face and, in a trembling voice, asked, "A...a...Anuj, are you my Bhanta? Why don't you say something—are you really Anuj?"

Anuj, choking back tears, replied, "Yes, my brother, I'm your Bhanta. Forgive me—I never went anywhere. The day they came to adopt me, they chose someone else because I was the smallest, and they wanted a tall boy. They refused to take me, and later, someone labeled me as Muslim. When nature made us human, it didn't distinguish between fair and dark, Hindu and Muslim, Parsi, Christian, or Buddhist—so why do humans live with such arrogance, when in the end, we all return to the same earth?"

Anuj continued, "But didn't you have eye surgery? You could see, right? When the warden told us, we were all so happy. No one was happier than me that my brother would finally see the world."

Vimal replied, "You're right, I could see for a while, but maybe God had already decided how long that would last."

Anuj asked, "But wait—when you were at the doctor's house, how did you end up here? The doctor was such a good man..."

Vimal explained how the doctor's wife mistreated him. "Madam liked you—she saw her own child in you. But for some reason, she could never accept me. When the doctor was home, I was treated well, but when he was away, Madam treated me worse than an animal." He also shared that only one of his eyes had been operated on, and that too didn't last—perhaps God never intended for him to see.

Hearing Anuj's story, Vimal was filled with rage, as if he would have lashed out at those children and the doctor's wife if they were in front of him. Anuj described that time as the darkest stain on his life—"Those were the black marks of my life, but they led me here." Vimal added that the red spots in his eyes had turned his world dark, too.

After hearing each other's stories, both were deeply saddened. "But now, we'll never leave each other's side—we promise," they said together.

*fig:*Guide (Anuj, becoming Vimal's eyes by supporting him on his shoulder)

The two became "charioteers" for each other—inseparable companions in every sense. They lived together, ate together, and went everywhere side by side.

Anuj would walk behind Vimal, acting as his eyes, while Vimal became Anuj's long legs, allowing them to cover great distances and accomplish all their tasks together. Though they still didn't have a proper place to live, people would call them "Vikram and Betaal," but none of this bothered them. They were happy, complementing each other, fulfilling the childhood promise they had made to always stand by one another.

Time kept moving forward, and they continued to support each other. Nearby, there was a spot where the temple priest and the mosque's Maulana used to gather. They would sit and discuss, often lamenting the state of society—how, in this greedy world, two religions could not coexist in life, yet after death, both were buried in the same earth at the cremation ground. Hindu and Muslim alike would be brought there, even though the selfish world had divided the cremation ground itself: on one side of a weak foundation lay the Muslim graves, and on the other, the Hindus. But who could explain to those narrow-minded people that, in the end, all bodies return to the same soil?

The Maulana would offer prayers for the deceased, while the priest performed Hindu rituals. The cremation ground was the only place where, after death, both Hindus and Muslims were brought together. In Hindu tradition, the body is given both fire and earth. Every day, an old, seemingly mad man would greet Anuj and Vimal with a "Namaste" and "Adaab." He wandered nearby and, when they sat, would sit a little distance away to listen to their conversations. If there was anything to eat or drink, the Maulana would share it with him too.

Nature has never discriminated against any living being. Air, water, and all resources needed for life are as much for animals and creatures as they are for humans—and so it remains to this day.

> "*Nature is that mother who never discriminates among her children; whether a child is a king or a pauper, she offers them equal love and resources. It is the petty and greedy minds of humans that have labeled this world as selfish, deceitful, and full of discrimination.*"

One day, someone bought the place where Anuj and Vimal lived, and there was talk of building a grand, luxurious hotel on that land. Their relationship with Maulana Sahib and the temple priest was good, as sometimes the Maulana and the priest themselves arranged food for them. When they became homeless, Maulana Sahib suggested, "Why don't you both set up your tin shack here in the cremation ground? If anyone comes, you can help dig graves or assist in other ways, and you'll earn a little money and get something to eat." The priest agreed, saying, "As for food, just as we eat, the Lord will provide for you too." Their new home was now in the cremation ground, far from the world and society. The mad old man's routine remained the same—he would come, listen to their conversations, eat if there was something, and then wander off.

One day, when the old madman didn't show up, Anuj and Vimal grew concerned and went looking for him. They found him injured, lying near a garbage heap. They took him to the hospital, got him treated, and brought him back to stay with them. They cared for him, but as soon as he recovered, he ran off again—he felt trapped living with them. Yet, every evening at mealtime, he would return.

fig: People beating the madman .

The doms (traditional cremation ground workers) who lived there did not like Anuj and Vimal staying in the cremation ground. Sometimes, they would get angry at them. One day, things went too far—the doms tore down Anuj and Vimal's entire tin shack and threw it away. The doms resented that Anuj and Vimal did any work out of service, while the doms would not do anything without payment. Moreover, the doms couldn't tolerate the growing closeness between Anuj, Vimal, the priest, and the Maulana.

A few days later, the doms decided to drive Anuj and Vimal out for good. They were even ready to kill them.

They destroyed their shelter and attacked them. Anuj and Vimal tried to call for help from the priest and Maulana, but the doms covered their mouths so they couldn't shout, and beat them severely. The madman, seeing this from a distance, rushed to help but was also injured in the process. Anuj and Vimal pleaded, "Please let us go—we'll leave and never come back," but the doms said, "If we let you go today, you'll just come back and settle here again." They chased and beat them, and the poor madman fell, wounded, trying to save them. Somehow, Anuj and Vimal managed to escape and hid in a safe place, going hungry and thirsty for several days, too afraid to come out.

One day, a man carrying bags of food—perhaps delivering to a hostel or office—was passing by. Sitting by the roadside, a helpless, hungry man looked at him as if he were God. Suddenly, one of the food bags fell from the group, but the delivery man didn't notice and kept walking. The mad old man, sitting nearby, thanked God and picked up the bag. He ate some and, holding the rest, started to leave. Suddenly, a dog chased him, barking. Running from the dog, the bag slipped from his hands and fell under a bridge.

Anuj and Vimal were hiding under that bridge, avoiding people. When they saw the bag of food, they felt it was a sign from God, as they had just prayed for food moments before. Anuj quickly grabbed the bag, and they were overjoyed to find food. Thanking God, they ate together. Vimal was not feeling well and couldn't get up, but together, supporting each other, they eventually came out. They were still haunted by the fear that people might kill them. Gradually, as they became able to live among people again, they started working hard as laborers.

The priest, familiar with their character, gave them a piece of empty land next to the temple to live on. Because he understood their nature, he had no hesitation in helping them.

One day, some naive Hindu youths, offended by the alarm sounding from the mosque, began to dismantle the siren. This was because a political leader had commented on a news channel about Muslims praying five times a day, saying, "Will Allah not hear you unless you use a microphone? Our God listens to us even when we pray in our hearts, and He fulfills all our wishes. If Allah isn't listening, convert to Hinduism—your wishes will be fulfilled too." In retaliation, some Muslims sat on the road leading to the temple, blocking access for worshippers.

That same evening, some outsiders working at the hotel stole the donation box from the temple. The result was chaos—Hindu-Muslim riots erupted once again, leaving Anuj and Vimal homeless. In the riots, people began attacking each other. When they asked Anuj and Vimal about their religion and got no answer, they beat them too.

Vimal's health was deteriorating; he suffered daily, the pain stemming from an injury to his eye received during the beating at the cremation ground. One day, blood began to flow from his eyes. Anuj, alarmed, rushed him to the hospital. The doctor revealed that Vimal had cancer. The same blood clots that had once clouded his vision had now taken the form of cancer.

First, his sight was taken; now, he stood at death's door. On their way back from the hospital, the riotous crowd separated them. Vimal shouted and called for Anuj, but couldn't find him. Because of his small size, Anuj was trampled underfoot in the stampede; no one noticed as he was crushed. The mad old man tried to save him, shielding

Anuj with his own body like armor, but fate had other plans—both were trampled by the crowd. They were no longer of this world.

That mad old man was none other than Hamza's friend, Ramvilas, who, despite his unstable mental state, had unknowingly fulfilled the promise he had made to his dying wife—to protect and care for those children, even at the cost of his own life.

CHAPTER THREE

FAREWELL

Vimal lay helpless and injured on the roadside. After the riot ended, hospital vehicles arrived to collect the bodies. Those who lay there, lifeless and abandoned, were neither Hindu nor Muslim—they were simply human beings who no longer belonged to this world. Those who incite and participate in riots have no religion; they are a stain on the name of humanity. Hindus, after killing a handful of Muslims, believed their faith had become superior, and Muslims, after killing a few Hindus, thought they had proven their own faith's supremacy. But they do not realize that God, Allah, and the Lord are all one and the same; all holy scriptures teach only love and virtue. They never teach victory over religion, but over inhumanity—and that is why they are divine. When they look down and see people fighting in their names, they must surely regret having created this world.

fig: Vimal in police station asking about his friend

Vimal was found alive and taken to the hospital. The city had been scattered by the riots. A few days later, when Vimal returned, he went to the police station to file a missing person report for his friend. After repeated visits, the inspector, annoyed, shoved him out. Vimal had heard insults before, but this time the inspector's words cut deep: "He's probably dead, that little dwarf. We looked, didn't find him. Don't show your face here again, or you'll end up like those people lying there. What's your caste, what's your religion? Get lost, you one-eyed freak. Throw him out—if I see him again, he'll get the same treatment."

*fig:*The accident of helpless Vimal.

Just as a bullock cart without its driver goes astray and falls into a ditch, so was Vimal without Anuj—lost, directionless, and empty-hearted. No one came to help him. His condition grew worse; he stopped caring about food, and day by day, cancer consumed him. He grew weaker and weaker. The loss of his friend blinded not only his eyes but also his soul, leaving him wandering, stumbling, and hurting until one day, in an accident, he bid farewell to this cruel world.

Any form of discrimination is fatal to humanity. Humanity is the greatest religion. Just as the priest and the Maulana helped Anuj and Vimal at every step, if everyone in society thought like them, Anuj and Vimal would never have been separated. It is our responsibility not to act in the name of religion, but to practice the humanity that true spirituality teaches us.

CHAPTER FOUR

"*Farewell is not just a word,*
But a silent promise of memories left behind.
A closing chapter, yet a beginning unseen,
Where hearts part but souls remain intertwined.
In every goodbye lies a hope—
That paths may cross once again,
That time will heal, and distance fade,
And love will find its way back home.
So with a heavy heart and a whispered prayer,
We say, "Alvida"—farewell, my friend,
Until we meet again, somewhere, somehow,
In the endless journey of life's embrace."

CHAPTER FIVE

THE UNION OF CHARIOTEERS

Life's journey is long and uncertain.
Sometimes, destiny brings together two travelers—
Each incomplete on their own,
But together, they become each other's charioteer.
One becomes the eyes, the other the feet;
One lends courage, the other hope.
In a world divided by walls of religion, caste, and
prejudice,
Their bond becomes a living lesson—
That true companionship knows no boundaries.
Like Krishna to Arjuna,
A real charioteer does not just steer the path,
But stands by in every storm,
Guiding, supporting, and never letting go.
Anuj and Vimal, two souls battered by fate,
Found in each other the missing piece—
A friendship that defied society's cruelty,
A partnership that turned pain into strength,
And loneliness into love.

CHAPTER SIX

"The Union of Charioteers is not just a meeting of two
people,
But the coming together of hope and resilience—
A reminder that, in the end,
It is not blood, caste, or creed that matters,
But the hand you hold, and the heart that walks beside
you."
- Manju Ashish Buddhaghosh

Writer's Introduction

Name : Manju Ashish Buddhaghosh (Screen Writer, Artist, Engineer)

DOB: 13th April 1998

Education: Bachelor's degree in Technology (Information Technology)

Profession: Software Engineer, Artist

Grand Father: Mr. Babu Ram Gautam (Retired Principal)

Father: Dr. Ashish Kumar Gautam

(National-level award winner, author, teacher, thinker)

Mother: Mrs. Manju Gautam (Teacher)

Genres: Article, Story & Screenplay Writing

Interests: Listening to music, Watching cinema, Design, and Traveling

Contact Address: Basthanwa Nedula, Basti 272130 (Uttar Pradesh),

Contact: +919918293747, thebuddhaghosh@gmail.com

"When humanity becomes our religion,
And compassion our language,
Every lost traveler finds a charioteer,
And every journey finds its meaning.
- Buddhaghosh"

www.ingramcontent.com/pod-product-compliance
Lightning Source LLC
Chambersburg PA
CBHW031512150726
47990CB00007B/2980